Megan's Mare

LYNN HALL

Megan's Mare

CHARLES SCRIBNER'S SONS · NEW YORK

Copyright © 1983 Lynn Hall

Library of Congress Cataloging in Publication Data
Hall, Lynn.   Megan's mare.
Summary: Eleven-year-old Megan, daughter of a
Yorkshire horse trainer, finding she has a special bond
with the beautiful problem mare Berry, determines to
help her overcome her fear of wooden bridges.
[1. Horses—Fiction. 2. Horses—Training—
Fiction] I. Title.
PZ7.H1458Me   1983   [Fic]   83-3009
ISBN 0-684-17874-5

3 5 7 9 11 13 15 17 19   FK/C   20 18 16 14 12 10 8 6 4 2

Printed in the United States of America.

Megan's Mare

When I look back on my life, which I seldom have time to do, it seems to fall into segments according to horses. First there was Terrance, my mother's old hunter. I taught myself to stand and walk by pulling myself up on Terrance's tail and groping about his legs. Or so they tell me.

Then there was Tiger, a little dun native pony. He was a lovely sandy color with a black stripe down his back and a mop of a mane. And as I outgrew him, there were others.

At the time, I took my life for granted, as all children do. I assumed everyone lived as I did. But later I realized how incredibly lucky I was to have been born into my family.

We had a bit of a farm up in the Yorkshire dales. Back then it was all lovely rolling fields and meadows crisscrossed with stone walls and hawthorne hedges, and misted over with heather. The roads were soft dirt tracks just right for galloping about on, with few motorcars to smell up the place and frighten the horses.

As I grew older, my dad gradually became less farmer and more horse trainer. He'd always had a way with them, and so had Mum, and apparently his reputation got about. Folks began sending him their problem animals for schooling. Mum worked at it, too. Some of the horses responded to her better than to Dad. Even I got into the business from time to time, when someone sent us a pony too small to carry an adult. Then I did the riding, and Dad yelled directions at me from the paddock fence.

It didn't earn us much of a living, but it was a grand life.

Then Dad began combing the local livestock sales in search of likely-looking horses. His idea of "likely" was an animal that was thin and poor and ill used. They could always be bought cheaply, given some good care and a bit of training to iron out any vices they might have, and sold at a considerable profit later on.

One evening Dad answered a knock on the door, read the note that was handed to him, and said to Mum, "I've a telephone message, love. Be back in a shake." And he left.

The nearest telephone was at the pub in the village two miles away. People wanting my dad would phone the pub and leave a message, and Dad would go down, return the call, and come home a few hours later, grinning and smelling of ale.

I was eleven years old, and nobody's fool. After Dad left, I said, "We could have our own telephone, couldn't we, Mum? The line goes right past here. I think Dad likes it better this way. It gives him an excuse to sit around that place, evenings, drinking with his friends."

Mum looked at me and smiled calmly.

I said, "Why does he need an excuse? All the other men in the neighborhood spend their evenings down there, and they don't pretend it's because of the telephone. Why doesn't Dad just go down there?"

She bit off her sewing thread and knotted it

3

expertly. "T'wouldn't be as much fun for him, if he didn't think he was putting one over on us. Don't you spoil it for him."

I agreed, but I had my suspicions. I was pretty sure that most of the messages the pub owner's son brought were fakes. But that evening there had been a genuine phone call.

When Dad came home he said to me, "Megan, there's a horse coming on the morning train tomorrow. You'll have to go fetch it home. And mind you lead it home. Don't try to ride it. It's a bit of a bad actor, apparently."

To Mum he said, "That was Greenlanes riding stable, down by Harrogate. Wanted me to see what I could do with the mare. Said she's pretty as a picture and all the young riding students want to ride her, but she's gotten unmanageable, and even the owners can't handle her now. Won't cross bridges, bolting for the barn, that sort of thing."

Mum nodded. "Sounds like that old bad combination, a smart horse and a lot of timid beginner riders. No proper discipline. Shouldn't be too much of a job to get the mare straightened out. Did you buy her, or are we training her for the stable?"

4

"We left it a bit up in the air," Dad said, settling into his chair. "They'd like to have her back if we can break her of her vices, but they don't want to spend a lot on training fees. It's not a very prosperous stable, I take it. We'll just see how it goes."

Next morning I got my barn chores done in good time and set out for the train station two miles away. It was a grand morning, early June and warm, and the air was rich with the smells of wildflowers and succulent grass. New lambs bounced along with me as I walked, them on their side of the hedge and me on mine, but sharing the morning anyway.

At the railway station I sat on the baggage wagon drumming my heels against its tires and exchanging news and gossip with Henry, the station master. Then the train was there, filling the place with its size and noise and excitement. It hissed to a silent stop finally, and the door of the baggage car rolled open.

Get me out of here.

I felt the words in my head, but I didn't know where they came from. It was just a feeling, suddenly, that seemed to come into me from the direction of the baggage car, a dark wave of fear and anger and the feeling of someone calling, "Get me out of here."

The sensation was new to me, and it left me shaken. But there was no time to think about it now. The ramp was in place and the baggage-man was leading a horse into view, in the square of sunlight that illuminated the inside of the car.

"Ohh," I breathed.

She was a picture. A small, fine-boned mare, a strawberry roan, light rose in color, with a silver mane and tail, and her legs and head shaded to a deep rust red. Her head was thrown back, her nostrils flaring, her eyes white-rimmed and staring in terror.

Then her stare collided with mine, and I knew. The message had come from her.

I waited for the baggageman to lead her down the ramp. The mare put one foot on the wooden ramp, then backed away from it, terrified. He urged, she balked. The more he urged, the more grimly the little red mare refused.

I was about to come up the ramp myself, to see if I could lead her down, when the mare made her own decision. She lowered her head and backed swiftly into the shadows of the car, then burst out toward me, clattering, leaping out into the air and landing wide-eyed and wide-legged on the ground. Her feet hadn't touched the ramp.

Instinctively I grabbed the rope before she

had time to collect her wits and bolt away. "There now," I soothed her with my voice, "don't you feel like a bloody fool, behaving that way? Never mind, we'll teach you. Come along then. We'll go home."

I signed Henry's delivery receipt and led the little horse out onto the road toward home. When we were out of sight of the station, and anyone who might tell Dad, I jumped onto the mare's back and settled in for the ride home. I remembered Dad's instructions to lead her home, but it went against every fiber of my being, every instinct in my nature, to lead a horse for two miles when there was that lovely glossy back just waiting for my bottom.

She went along quietly for me. She seemed worn out by the tension of the train journey, and walked along calmly, nodding her head in rhythm with her step and letting her ears relax.

I relaxed, too, and stroked the sunset-pink neck and thought about the mare. Berry, her name was. Dad had said last night that she was a five-year-old, half-thoroughbred, half-New Forest pony. As I studied her I could almost read her pedigree in the lines of her body. Her head and neck showed a thoroughbred elegance, but her body was short-coupled and her legs a bit more sturdy than a thoroughbred's. And her size, not much more than thirteen hands, was pure New Forest.

Her size was a godsend for me. She was too small to carry Dad, even too small for Mum to ride comfortably, since Mum stood close to six feet tall herself and felt out of place on any horse less than a sixteen-hand hunter.

And so, I figured, Berry would be mine to work with. I loved her already. I loved her beauty, her silvery-rose color, her miniature-thoroughbred elegance. But then I found something to love about almost all of the horses that passed through my life.

About a mile from home we came to a bridge across a narrow stream. It was an old arching stone bridge, earth-floored, with grass growing along the edges. As we approached, I debated whether to try to ride her across the bridge and risk having her balk, or to ride off the road and wade her across the stream. Attempting the bridge would be dangerous, not because I might be thrown but because I was not prepared to force her across, if she should refuse. I had no whip or stick or spurs, and no bit in her mouth, nothing but the halter and lead rope. Very poor controls with which to go into battle with a stubborn horse.

One of Dad's firmest rules, in training horses, was that we must never allow the horse to get the better of us. Never give a command unless we were in a position to enforce it. Never allow a horse to feel that he was boss. I knew that if I rode Berry at the bridge, and she refused to cross it, I would be unable to force her across and she would have won the battle. This would prove to her that she was dominant over me, as she apparently had been over the children at the riding stable. I should never be able to train her properly, after that, because she would not respect me.

So, reluctantly, because I was curious to know if I could have ridden her over the bridge, I turned her off of the road and we splashed through the stream.

Just before home came into view I slipped down from Berry's back, brushed her hairs from my trouser legs, and led her sedately into the farmyard.

Dad was schooling a young hunter over the jumps in the low meadow, and Mum and the veterinary had their heads together over old Terrance, who had chronic foot problems. He was past thirty, and had belonged to Mum ever since she was my age.

I put Berry in an empty stall and brought her food and water, then stood outside the stall door with the sun on my back, watching her.

Our stable was a long, L-shaped building with each stall opening directly onto the cobblestone yard. Our house formed the third side of the square. It was quite old, four or five hundred years in parts, but it was a dear old place, made of dressed flint and dark timbers and creamy plaster, with vines that grew all the way to the roof tiles in places. Now and then Mum tried to grow flowers in the side gardens, but she was more interested in the horses than in weeding flower beds, and it seldom came to anything. Once when I was ill Mum turned Tiger loose in the side garden so that I could pet him through my window, and the flower beds were never quite the same after that. Tiger could eat the blossom off a rose so neatly that no thorn ever touched his lips.

Eventually the veterinary drove away and Dad brought his hunter in from the jumps, and he and Mum came to see Berry.

"Bit small, isn't she?" Dad said, frowning.

"Not for some people," I chirped. He gave me a wry look.

Mum said, "Did she lead home all right, Megan?"

"She didn't give me a bit of trouble." I saw Mum twisting her head back to look at the seat of my pants, then raising her eyebrow at me. I turned slightly away from her too-knowing eyes and went on.

"She didn't want to come down the ramp from the baggage car, though. Seemed to be afraid of it. Finally she took a run at it and jumped all the way to the ground. Missed the ramp completely."

Dad said, "Hmm," and nodded. "She's a smart little thing, I've no doubt. These thoroughbred-pony cross-breds are like that sometimes. They've got the sensitivity of the thoroughbred and the wiliness of a pony. They can be tough as nails to train, these smart ones. They challenge you every step of the way, and they watch for any sign of weakness on your part, and then they take advantage. But if you can master them, ah, then you have something. Spirit and brains and heart and sensitivity."

"Will you let me work with her?" I asked.

Dad snorted. "I expect I'll have to. Your mum and I, either one, would be too heavy for that fine-boned little frame. But you're not to ride her until I can be there to give you a hand. I won't have you taking chances with her, understand?"

Meekly I nodded and turned my horse-marked trousers to the stable wall.

That evening we turned Berry out in the small meadow behind the house, to let her stretch her legs and relax and graze.

Next morning at breakfast Dad said, "I'm going to work Grahame over the jumps for a bit, Megan. Then we'll have a go at the little roan mare. You can be getting her caught up and groomed, and see if there's a bridle to fit her. Let's try a mullen-mouth pelham bit first."

"Spot on, chief," I said, and scraped up the last of my porridge on my way to the sink. I ran out the back way and across the wild-grown back garden to the low stone wall of the meadow. Berry was grazing a little distance away.

I called and she ignored me. Understandable enough.

I climbed the wall and approached her. She watched, calmly, until I was close, then turned and trotted away.

All right, still understandable. I pulled up a handful of grass and followed her, offering the grass.

Again she watched until I drew near, then moved away.

She was playing games with me. I knew it and she knew it. She had the run of a lush meadow, and she had no desire to be caught and ridden. I knew that if I ran after her she would gallop away, faster than I could run. I also knew that if I gave up and let her win, I would never be her master. I ran to the stable for a pan of oats and came back, determined to get her.

She looked at the oats, and she looked at me. Suddenly I had the feeling that she was laughing at me, at my transparent attempt to bribe her into captivity with oats.

She turned and strolled away.

I followed.

Around and across the meadow we walked. When I stopped, Berry stopped, too, and put down her head to graze. But when I came closer than two or three yards, we were off again, walking, she with calm amusement, I with grim patience.

Dad appeared at the wall and watched for a while. "That's it," he called. "You can outlast her. I'll go lunge the yearlings for a bit. Give me a call when you're ready to ride."

I nodded at him and muttered, "If we haven't both died of old age before then."

The morning passed. The sun grew hot. My shirt stuck to my back and my legs grew wobbly weak. I hoped the mare was as uncomfortable as I was, but she appeared to be enjoying our four-hour stroll back and forth, 'round and 'round the small meadow.

Some time around midday Mum brought me a sausage roll and a jug of cold water. I ate and drank, and trudged on.

"Keep it up," Mum cheered from her cool seat on the shady wall. "She's bound to give in sooner or later."

This time I muttered something I'd have been punished for saying, if Mum had heard.

It was past two o'clock when Berry finally

stopped and stood and allowed me to come up to her. I gripped her halter and we looked long and hard at one another. The challenge was still there in her eyes. Faking affection I was far from feeling at this point, I crooned to her and rubbed her neck and praised her. I led her to the pan of oats and gave her a few bites.

Then I turned her loose.

Mum and Dad were both watching from the wall, by this time. Mum called, "What did you let her loose for, you goose? You just spent six hours catching her."

But Dad understood. "Good show, Meg," he called.

As soon as I was old enough to listen, but still too young to understand much of what he said, Dad talked to me about training horses. I think he liked to hear his theories voiced, and I was his only audience. Mum had her own theories and would get impatient at having to listen to his.

I didn't always understand what he told me, but one thing he said, early on in our talks, did stay with me. Think like the horse thinks, he told me. You've got to put yourself inside that animal's brain, see things the way he sees them, and *then* outfox him.

So today I thought as Berry would think. If being caught always led to being ridden, then being caught was to be avoided. But if being caught meant praise and petting and a snack of oats, and then freedom again, all good things and no bad things, then being caught was not something to be avoided after all.

Berry walked away from me and I forced my aching legs to follow her. This time it took less than an hour to catch her. Again she was praised and given oats, and again she was released.

I rolled into the long cool grass under a tree, and dozed and rested while Berry grazed nearby. When I felt ready, I got up, walked to her, and caught hold of her halter. It might have been my imagination, but this time her eyes seemed to glow more softly, with perhaps even a glimmer of respect.

When Berry allowed me to catch her without a fuss next morning, I was triumphant. The battle was mine.

The battle, perhaps, but it proved to be only the opening skirmish. The war was yet to be fought.

We started in the small paddock with Dad watching from the fence. Before Berry had carried me more than a half-dozen steps I realized that our illicit ride home from the train had given me a poor sample of this little horse. Today, rested and well fed, under saddle and bridle, Berry became a feather of a horse. She arched her neck and came up on that bit like a professional, so that the touch of her sensitive mouth was in my hands, but not the weight of her head. The curve of her body fit my legs, and, riding her, I felt beautiful.

After a bit I rode over to Dad and said, "She must not have been a riding stable horse very long. She's not the least bit hard-mouthed."

He turned and beckoned to Mum, who was on her way to the stable. To me he said, "It's obvious the mare doesn't need any paddock work. I want you to take her out for a good long trek, find some bridges. Ev, why don't you go along with her on Terrance."

I didn't mind his sending Mum along. I knew what he was doing, using Terrance as a steadying influence on Berry. He often used Terrance as a teacher with a frightened young horse. Terrance was a huge, rawboned chestnut with age-hollows about his eyes and a good deal of gray on his face. The sideboard in our dining room was lined with trophies Mum and Terrance had won, steeplechasing, when they were both young.

Even now, as we jogged down the summer

road, Terrance looked eagerly at the fences we passed, hoping for one more chase over fields and fences in a pack of excited horses and gaily shouting riders.

One of the nice things about riding with Mum was that it was almost like riding alone. She hummed, sometimes sang, sometimes directed a remark to her horse, but almost never spoke to me. That left me free to savor my horse and the morning.

Berry bucked a few times when we began cantering, but it was no more than high spirits, and she settled down willingly enough when I insisted. Our first real test came a mile from home, at the bridge that I had avoided on the ride home from the station.

I braced myself for a battle, but the little mare trotted across the bridge at Terrance's side without so much as a hesitation. At the far side, we stopped.

"Well now," Mum said, "that was a bit of barley-cake, wasn't it? Want to try it without Terrance?"

"Good idea." I turned Berry around and headed her over the bridge, away from Terrance.

Again she trotted willingly across the grassy earth floor of the ancient bridge. Mum and I shrugged at each other, and rode on.

We jumped a very low gate and had an easy canter across a sheep meadow. Then, in respect for Terrance's years, we slowed to an ambling walk and entered a track through a beech wood. The trees here were so tall and so dense at the top that they shaded out the undergrowth and left a forest floor carpeted with mosses and wild-flowers. The sun came through in shafts and made it seem a magic place.

Midway through the wood was a stream spanned by a rattly wooden bridge. It was flat with the ground, and no more than ten feet across, but there were spaces between the planks where the sparkling stream water showed through, and many of our horses were nervous about crossing it the first time.

This, I knew, would be a sterner test for Berry than the solid, earth-covered bridge on the road. I gathered my determination and set her at the bridge just behind the steady Terrance.

Ca-lop, ca-lop, ca-lop, Terrance crossed the bridge.

Berry placed one hoof on the first board, then drew back.

I felt fear sifting into my mind like a dark fog. And yet it was not my fear.

"Come along, love, it's perfectly safe. Terrance went across, and you can, too," I told her. I tried desperately to block out the terror that was threatening to swamp my mind.

Berry backed, turned, tried to spin away from my hold on her. I wouldn't let her. Using my legs as hard as I could, I pushed her toward the bridge. She planted her feet and froze. I turned her in small circles to break the balk, then aimed her at the bridge again.

Suddenly she began backing. She backed swiftly for several steps, then leaped toward the bridge.

"Good girl," I shouted.

She gathered herself and leaped, a magnificent broad jump that cleared the bridge and landed us safely on the other side.

Joining Mum, I grinned ruefully. "I wonder which one of us won that round."

"You got her across it," Mum said.

"Yes, but she didn't step on it. I expect we'll have to call it a tie, this time."

We rode on, Mum whistling some unrecognizable tune, and me trying not to think of that curious dark fear, so like the feeling that had come over me in the train station when Berry arrived.

After that day I rode out alone on Berry every morning. As it became routine, she began to show some of her riding stable attitude. The first day or so it was pleasant for her. But when it became an everyday job to carry me about the countryside she began to object. She had already learned, through experience at the stable with inexperienced riders, that if she balked and fussed, the ride usually ended and she was turned out to pasture again. It was not so much that she was lazy as it was that she was smart, and she had learned that people could be tricked.

She was smart and she was stubborn, but then so was I. When she planted her feet and refused to go, I turned her toward home, then quickly turned her again, sometimes spinning her in a circle several times until she was tired and dizzy and willing to go in any direction I aimed her.

She quit balking and switched to anothe

tactic—backing up. We had almost reached the edge of the village one afternoon when Berry stopped in the middle of the road and began to go backward.

"All right, you bloody cow," I swore, "you want to back up, we'll back up."

I let her carry me backward until she was ready to stop. But I wouldn't let her stop. I tightened the reins and commanded, "Back."

Back we went, up the hill, around the curve, past the Overbys' and the Jacksons'. Michael Jackson strolled past us, heading toward town with his sheepdog at his heels.

"Morning, Michael," I said as we backed past him.

"Mornin', Meg." He turned to look curiously after us.

On we went, backward.

Sheep appeared around Berry's legs; the Kentwoods' flock was being moved from one sheep run to another. Berry tensed as the gray tide separated and flowed around her, to pour itself together in front of us.

"Morning, Mr. Kentwood. Lovely day, isn't it?"

24

The old man just stared at us and shook his head.

By now Berry was asking for release. Her legs were tired of the unaccustomed strain of going backward. Finally, after more than a mile, I let her stop.

"Now will you go forward?" I asked her.

We went forward.

After that I thought the war was won. Most horses would have conceded leadership before now. But I underestimated Berry's stamina and stubbornness.

Her next maneuver was much more dangerous than balking or backing. She began bolting toward trees with low-hanging branches, attempting to knock me off. It was a common enough pony's trick, but I was dismayed to find it in my beautiful Berry's repertoire. The truth of the matter was that I was in love with the little rose-and-silver devil.

I was already determined to talk Dad into keeping her for me. Since I'd outgrown Tiger I hadn't had a horse of my own, and according to my way of figuring, I had more than earned one, with all the help I'd given Dad in training ponies.

25

Mum had Terrance and Dad had Behemoth, his mammoth bucket-footed hunter. So it was only just that I should have Berry, and I felt confident that Dad could be talked around to it.

But only if I could break her of this new and dangerous tree-branch business. Even my parents' casual confidence in my horsemanship probably wouldn't stretch to cover that sort of risk. So far neither of them had seen Berry do it, but it was just a matter of time.

There was one tree especially suited for Berry's evil purpose, an oak with a strategically placed limb. So far I had escaped the limb by leaning low over her neck as she swept under it, but still she continued to try.

I rode her past the tree deliberately, hoping that eventually she would decide it was useless to try to knock me off. One afternoon we passed the tree seven times, back and forth, and every time we neared the tree she managed to snatch the bit in her teeth and dash toward the limb.

On the eighth pass my patience ran out. She dashed, and I hauled away on the rein, trying to turn her away from the tree. At the last second some instinct made me shift my weight to the other rein. She was caught off balance, and she cracked headlong into the tree trunk.

I flew head over teakettle onto the grass. When I regained my breath and rose, Berry was lying flat out on the grass.

"Oh, no, don't be dead," I cried.

She raised her head, shook it, stared at me with dazed eyes. I took her bridle and urged her up.

"Come up now, there's a love."

She staggered to her feet and stood, swaying. Gradually her body steadied and her eyes began to focus. She raised her head and looked at me.

She seemed overcome with awe.

The change in Berry's attitude was not so notice-
able to Mum and Dad since, before the tree
crash, they had only seen us ride away and come
home again a few hours later, day after day.
They had only my reports of, "She's coming
along," to go by.

But to me, knowing the truth about her
former behavior, Berry seemed a changed horse.
There were no more treacherous dashes toward
trees. She backed only when I asked her to, and
she balked almost never. Apparently, her colli-
sion with the tree convinced her, once and for
all, that I was more powerful than she was. And,

true to equine nature, she bowed to the superior authority and laid her trust in my hands.

From that point on our rides reverted to the mutual pleasure of that earlier ride. Having given me her trust, Berry became relaxed, supple as an athlete, and perfectly in tune with my hands, my legs, the shifting balance of my weight. Oh, we were a pair, the two of us, full of summer sunshine, full of ourselves.

On the first Sunday in August each year, our village holds a warm-up point-to-point. It's more like a fair than a horse race, but it's great fun and of course our family always rode in it. It was originally intended as a sort of practice run for the serious hunters, before the start of their season. But it had become a free-for-all. Anyone who could sit a horse joined in, and the mounts ranged from Shetland ponies to plow horses to a handful of actual hunters.

The three of us started out early that morning, I on Berry, Dad of course on Behemoth, and Mum on Feckless, a neat little bay Anglo-Arab who was in for training. It was a warm day but not as bad as it might have been; there was a cool north breeze.

The starting place was our village green. Standing in my stirrups, I counted at least thirty horses and ponies milling about. There was a delay of nearly an hour while we waited for any latecomers who might wander in. I used the time to remove Berry's saddle and let her rest in the shade beside the pub.

My friend Janey Oxberger appeared and came over to join me. She was as black-haired as her horse, a chunky Fell pony named Richard Lionheart, whom she had inherited from a string of older brothers and sisters. We seldom saw each other during the summer, because the horses kept me busy and Janey carried a heavy load of her own chores, but it was a good strong friendship nonetheless.

"I say, Meg, that's a beauty," she said, nodding to Berry. "Is she yours, or just here for training?"

"It's not decided yet. We took her for training, from a stable down by Harrogate, but they said they'd sell her, especially if the training bill ran too high, and I'm trying to talk Dad into letting me keep her. She's—"

We were interrupted by a shout for attention from Edward Overby, who was race chairman. I jumped to my feet and began saddling Berry.

"Attention, please. We'll begin in just a few minutes now. You all know the rules of the race, but I'll tell them to you one more time so we don't have any fights about it this year." He scowled down at two young men who had exchanged good-natured blows last year after the race.

"The rules are, same as always, you may open no gates, you may ride no more than a hundred yards down a road. You may not ride in any cultivated field nor through any farmyard. Other than that, you may go any way you want. First rider across the finish line at Minsterbury is the winner."

Janey and I rode into the pack at the starting line. I'd lost sight of Mum and Dad but it didn't matter. I tensed, and so did Berry. We had had no chance of winning the race, not against the great, leggy thoroughbred hunters that peppered the pack. The glory was in the ride and I leaned into it, into the silence and the pressure of the wait.

In accordance with some old and ridiculous

pretense that this was a hunt, the starting cry was "View-hallooooo—"

It sent us leaping forward, past the pub and over a low rail fence into Overby's sheep run. The smaller ponies went down-fence a short distance to a low spot where they could hop over safely.

After the first burst of speed most of us slowed to a hand gallop. It was six miles to Minsterbury over hilly country, with a score of fences, hedges, and streams to be jumped along the way. It was a test of endurance more than speed, and I didn't intend to wear Berry out in the first mile.

Across the meadow we sailed, over a stone wall and into the next field. I knew the way well from previous races and from my own rambling rides. Although it was a casual neighborhood point-to-point, and all in fun, it was a good course. None of the jumps were high or dangerous, and in most places the more timid riders, or the smaller ponies, could detour to a gap in the hedge, or a downed rail in the fence. They wouldn't be among the winners that way, but they'd have a lovely gallop and come in safely at the end.

Although I had no hope of winning the race I chose the most direct route for Berry, straight across the fields and fences. We made our leaps with the best of the hunters, or close behind them.

Berry loved it. She flung herself over rail and rock and hawthorne hedge, and I could feel her joy. About midway through the course I looked around. Dad was well ahead of me with the leaders; Mum was off to the side but going along well. Janey had disappeared somewhere behind me. Richard Lionheart was getting up in years, and she'd undoubtedly pulled him in to give him a breather.

Suddenly I thought of something. The Minsterbury bridge. It was a plank bridge, too long for Berry to leap as she had the little bridge in our beech wood.

And there was no way around it. Steep banks on either side fell away to the river below. We would have to go across.

The bridge approached, the horses came together in a tight pack. We were among them. They pressed Berry from behind, before, and either side.

Onto the bridge we clattered. Berry was

borne along helplessly. Suddenly the black terror filled my head.

I saw a jagged plank and a hole in the ground opening beneath me. I felt a tilting up, and total terror. And death.

We were across the bridge and galloping into the village, under the finish line rope. Still dazed from the vision, I automatically drew Berry down to a jog and walked her gently up and down the street to let her muscles ease up. She was winded and dripping sweat, but still high-headed.

I shook my head to clear it and looked around. Riders were still coming. I must have been in the first seven or eight, I figured, and all the others were big thoroughbreds. Mum was coming in now on her Anglo-Arab, and a few minutes later Janey appeared, with a handful of young children on small ponies.

The winner received his silver cup and much shouting and back-thumping. Dad grinned at his third-place ribbon, and Mum blew her hair out of her face and congratulated me, and we all started toward our own village. It was a slow, leisurely ride, and it gave our horses time to unwind without muscle cramps. We followed the road, some walking their horses, some riding, but everyone flushed and happy.

Mum came along beside me and said, "You must have got Berry over the Minsterbury bridge. Did she fight you?"

"She didn't have a chance. We were surrounded. She had to go over or be trampled."

"Good, then. Maybe that's what she needed."

I was silent. And I was thankful that the road home didn't cross that bridge. The unexplainable terror that filled my mind was still with me. This time I couldn't ignore it. Something was happening between Berry and me, something beyond my understanding, beyond my imagination.

Dad was so pleased with his placing in the point-to-point, and with the good showing Berry and I made, that it was easy to talk him into letting me keep her. Before her arrival Dad, or sometimes Mum, had mentioned from time to time that Megan should have a mount of her own, and I'd agreed. But I hadn't pressed the matter. The place was always full of horses to ride and care for, so the need for my own horse hadn't been a painful one.

But after a summer on Berry I'd have been heartbroken to lose her. She was mine and I was hers, and Mum and Dad were wise enough to see that.

As we spent more and more time together a curious bond began to grow between Berry and me. It was something separate from affection, although I loved her mightily and she was a more than usually affectionate horse. This was a closeness of minds. I don't know how to explain it, but it existed.

On school mornings Berry remained at the low end of the back meadow, grazing with the other horses. But on Saturday and Sunday mornings, when I came out the back door after breakfast, she was always there by the fence, waiting for our ride. At first I assumed that she sensed the rhythm of two days, five days, two days, five days. But one Tuesday school was closed because of some problem with the heating, and there was Berry, waiting for me as I came out the back door. It happened again a few weeks later when a snowstorm brought another holiday.

I began to wonder. . . .

One night in December I woke suddenly in the darkness. My mother's voice came sharply through the wall. I got up and fumbled into my robe and met the two of them in the passage.

"What's the matter?" I asked, still groggy with sleep.

Mum was white-faced. "It's Terrance. He's dead."

She, too, was in pajamas and had obviously not been out of the house. I ran after her and Dad, calling, "How do you know?"

"I just know."

We all pulled on boots and wraps, and ran out across the cobbled yard to Terrance's box. Dad held up the lantern; it sent our shadows dancing on the stones of the stable wall.

Terrance was down in the straw. He was still. A film glazed his eyes.

Mum cried softly into Dad's lapels, and we all stood about patting one another and glancing down at the grand old horse. Then, gradually, we hugged and patted our way back to the kitchen. Dad settled Mum at the table and poked the fire alive under the tea kettle.

We kept our coats and boots on till the kitchen warmed up, and until we all had steaming mugs to wrap our fingers around. Mum was through sobbing by then and was down to just an occasional hiccup.

"Goodness knows it shouldn't have been a surprise," she said. "He was thirty-one, and long past ready to go."

"But how did you *know*?" I asked again.

She raised her head and looked back and forth from Dad to me. "I'm not sure whether I was awake or asleep. I might have dreamed it. But there was a picture in my mind, clear as could be. Terrance standing there in the sunlight, looking like he used to when he was young. He was staring right at me, and I had the—sensation —that he was telling me good-bye. And I woke up and I knew he was dead."

I expected Dad to laugh it off, but he scooted his chair nearer the stove and said, "It happens. I've known of that sort of thing to happen."

"Really?" I gasped. I was thinking of Berry and me.

He nodded. "I've noticed between horses sometimes there'll be a special bond, a special closeness between two horses that are stable mates or just friends. If one is sick or frightened, the other one reacts the same way, even though they may be out of sight of each other completely."

"You mean like reading each other's minds?" I breathed.

"Something like that, I expect. It's not a thing I talk about much. People'd think I was a little crazy myself. But it's a fact, and I'll wager that lots of other folks who work with animals have seen it, too."

I leaned closer to Dad, my tea cooling unnoticed in my hands. "Can it happen between a horse and a person?"

Calmly Mum said, "Of course it can. It happened here tonight, or did you two forget? And it wasn't the first time."

She had our attention now.

"Don't you remember, Tom, how Terrance went off his feed when I was having Megan? I was in labor for almost two days," she explained to me, "and during the whole time Terrance paced about in his stall, sweating and refusing to eat. Old Jack Mathers was helping out then, and he was so worried, remember, Tom? Kept dosing poor Terrance with colic medicine. But the minute Meg was born, Terrance settled down and began to eat."

We all looked at one another in the silent, dark kitchen.

Finally, with an equal mixture of reluctance and eagerness, I said, "I think Berry and I can do that."

Their silence urged me on. "It happens when

she has to go over a bridge. Not the earth bridge out here on our road, but any wooden bridge. I get this sort of—fear—only it's not me that's afraid. It's as though Berry's fear somehow gets into my head. And last summer at the point-to-point when she had to go over the Minsterbury bridge I got the fear, and I also got a picture. In my head. It was this round black hole and broken boards right under our feet, and I felt as though I was tipping over backward, and there was death . . . ."

They looked at me, not with the superior skepticism I'd dreaded, but thoughtfully.

Finally Mum said, "It sounds to me as though Berry must have had some sort of bad scare in her past, and going over wooden bridges reminds her of it."

"And if you two are on the same mental wavelength, so to speak," Dad said, "she's broadcasting the memory and you're receiving it. If a radio can do it, isn't it possible that a mind can do it, too?"

Mum drained her cup and stood up. "Well, it's a fascinating subject, but it is the middle of the night, and we've all got work to do in the

41

morning. Best we get some sleep. Megan, I think you'd better stay home from school tomorrow. We're going to have to bury Terrance."

"He's not going to the knacker's, then?" I asked.

Dad stood close to Mum and put his arm around her shoulder. "Would we let your mum's friend go for dog food and glue? No, he'll be buried in the pasture. We can shovel the snow off and have a bonfire to thaw the ground so we can dig. I expect Jack and Ed and one or two of his boys will give us a hand. Off to bed now, Megan."

After that night I thought a lot about the possibility of two minds exchanging thoughts without words. I thought about Berry and me, and I loved the idea that there was a special, almost mystical closeness between us. I became obsessed with the need to find out about her past, to find out whether there had indeed been an accident resembling the picture I'd seen in my head at the Minsterbury bridge.

I wrote a letter to the stable at Harrogate, explaining who I was and asking whether Berry had ever had an accident on a bridge during the time they owned her. I worded the letter carefully to make it sound as though I were seeking help with the problem of getting her to cross bridges.

It seemed an endless time, but eventually a letter came for me, postmarked Harrogate. I grabbed it and ran to Berry's box, where I sat on her manger to read.

Dear Miss Dodson:

I was pleased to hear from you, and to know that Berry is happy in her new home. We here at Greenlanes always thought she was such a pretty little thing, and so intelligent. Unfortunately, the intelligent horses often make poor school horses, since they do tend to overpower the beginning students a bit.

To the best of my knowledge she had no accidents here involving bridges, simply because none of us was ever able to get her across a bridge. It's possible that something might have happened with one of the students that we don't know about, but it's not likely. Berry wasn't used in the trekking string. She was too undependable. So I don't believe that any of our students ever rode her out away from the stable, unattended. However, it is a possibility.

I've checked back in our records and found

the name of the dealer who sold Berry to us, in case you'd like to contact him. It was J.R. Sloane, Number Two, Peach Lane, York.

Good luck and best wishes,
Marion Stout
Greenlanes Stables, Harrogate

I sighed and stared at Berry's face, close beside my leg as she munched her afternoon hay. How was I ever going to find out what secrets were locked inside that russet head?

"By writing another letter," I muttered. "And waiting again."

I wrote to J.R. Sloane at York, describing Berry and asking for the name of the person from whom he had bought her.

There was no answer.

It was a warm, wet, turning-green Saturday in
March when Mr. Fergus arrived. Berry and I had
been for a romp in the sheep meadow near the
road when I looked up and noticed a little man
in a pony trap, stopped at the edge of the road.

He seemed to be waiting for a chance to ask
directions, so I rode over. Berry and I were both
a bit mud-splashed and breathless. You can't go
galloping across a sheep run in March and stay
tidy. I knocked the worst of it off my face with
my sleeve and said, "Have you lost your way?"

Only then did I notice how intently the man
was looking at Berry. His clothes and the whole

45

look of the man and the pony trap proclaimed him a farmer, probably quite poor but as clean as his profession allowed.

He didn't answer me, but wrapped his pony's lines about the whip holder and stepped down. "Hello, there, little dearie," he said softly. But it was Berry he spoke to, not me. He stroked her face, and I thought I saw a glimmer of wet around his eyes.

Finally he looked up at me and said, "Would you be a Miss Megan Dodson, by any chance?"

"Yes. How did you—"

He pulled from his pocket a letter, and I could see that it was the one I had written to Mr. Sloane, in York. Then he touched his hat in a gesture of respect that was especially sweet considering that I must have looked like a street urchin, all mud-splashed and straggle-haired.

"I'm James Fergus, from over by Haxby. This used to be my pony." He patted Berry's face with his stiff brown fingers. "I didn't come to try to get her back," he went on quickly. I must have looked concerned. "I only wanted to see that she was in a good spot. Not being abused, don't you know."

Here was the answer, I sang silently. "Come

along home, then," I said. "You've had a long drive. We'll put your pony up and talk."

Twenty minutes later Mr. Fergus's pony was unhitched and comfortable in our stable next to Berry, and Mr. Fergus and I were seated in the kitchen, in the comfortable chairs on either side of the fire. When Mum appeared from the stable I let her know, with wordless moves of my head, that this was my company, so she contented herself with welcoming Mr. Fergus and reminding me that there was a fresh tin of biscuits. I made the tea and fetched the biscuits, and then we settled in to talk.

"How did you happen to come looking for Berry?" I asked. It was all the priming Mr. Fergus needed.

"I'd been in to the city, to York, on a bit of farm business, you see, and I thought I'd stop around at Sloane's to ask about Berry. My children had been after me to find out what happened to her. Sloane had had your letter, and he passed it on to me. Said when he'd first got the letter he couldn't remember the little mare, and he just set the letter aside. Then me coming to ask after her, on top of your letter, it set him to thinking, especially when I told him my boy had brought him the pony in the dead of night. He'd reckoned she was stolen, you see. I expect that was why he so conveniently forgot about her, when you wrote. But when I told him the whole story, then he knew she hadn't been stolen, and he opened up a bit. Gave me your letter, in case I wanted to look you up. And as I say, my youngsters have been after me to come find out if Berry had a good home. We was all right attached to the little creature, miss."

"Then why did you sell her? And why in the middle of the night, to a dealer?"

"Well, miss, it happened like this." He swallowed his bite of biscuit and commenced to talk.

Berry's dam had been a little gray New Forest mare whose work it was to pull the family's pony trap, to do light work around the farm, and to carry as many of the Fergus children to school as would fit on her back. All of the family had a fondness for their animals. The sheep as well as the cows all had their names and their personalities, as did the barn cats who patrolled the farm.

48

The pony, Crumpet, was too old for having colts, but the Fergus fences weren't what they might have been, and a neighbor kept a thoroughbred stallion, and in due course the inevitable happened. Crumpet died giving birth, but the little strawberry roan filly thrived on her bottle feeding, and in a few years she had taken over her mother's duties with school children and trap.

Berry was raised as a puppy might have been, constantly handled and petted, and more than a bit spoiled. Her sire's thoroughbred sensitivity, her dam's solid good sense, and her continual contact with the family all combined to create, in Berry, an unusually quick and perceptive mind.

One day when Berry was a three year old, a group of young children, Ferguses and neighbors, went up onto the moors to play and, as they usually did, they took Berry along. They had all been forbidden to go beyond the edge of the moor at that place, because it was dangerous. Many years before, after the closing of the Cornish lead mines, a group of mining engineers had discovered a small deposit of lead in that area. They had sunk several exploratory shafts, then decided there was not enough lead to make mining worthwhile in that spot.

They covered the shafts with sturdy wooden covers about six feet square, and left them that way. At the time they seemed safe enough, but with the passing of the years the wood began to rot, and children were warned away from the area as a precaution.

But Bobby Fergus took the warning as a challenge. He led the group up onto the moors and scattered the children to search for a mine shaft. In short order one was found, a square of silvered wood planks half hidden by gorse and heather.

"I dare you to run across it," he shouted. No one took him up on the challenge.

"You do it," one of the others said.

Bobby ran across the planks. "See? I'm not afraid of it." He ran back across.

Berry lowered her head to nibble at the grass. On her back were the two smallest children in the group, Ian Fergus and little Jamie Gilroy, who was barely three.

"Do it again, slower this time," Janet Fergus urged. "Walk across."

"I will if you will."

"You do it first."

"All right, then." Bobby patted Berry's neck for luck, and started across. Berry followed.

The rotting boards gave way.

Bobby leaped to safety. The pony leaped, kicked, scrambled. Ian clutched her mane and screeched, but Jamie toppled over backward and disappeared into the mine shaft.

The terrified children ran for help, and families came with ropes and prayers, but there was no help for it. Jamie was dead.

After the first grief came the hard, angry questions. What were you children doing up there, where you oughtn't to be? Why were you playing on the mine shaft when you'd been told it was dangerous?

But the children had their story ready. Berry had bolted and run away, with Ian and Jamie on her back, and they had merely followed, trying to stop her. It wasn't that they wanted Berry to be blamed, but the death of a child was too much for Bobby, for any of them, to take responsibility for. They were all terrified—of their parents, of the police who might come and get them. Of God even.

In his grief, Jamie's father swore that the pony must be shot, and if Fergus wouldn't do it, he would come over himself and put the gun to Berry's head. Fergus stalled Mr. Gilroy with a promise of action the next day.

But that night, after the rest of the family was asleep, Fergus took Bobby to the darkened stable, where Berry was tied. Bobby was the only Fergus old enough to be trusted with the job, yet small enough to ride Berry. Fergus gave the boy careful directions to the horse dealer on Peach Lane in York.

When Gilroy came the next day, Fergus told him the pony had run away in the night. No one believed him, but it didn't matter. Berry was safely away.

After some months Bobby's conscience got the better of him, and he told his dad what had really happened. Fergus whipped his son for lying, as he felt he must do, but then the two of them cried together and decided that, later on, when the Gilroys' grief had abated somewhat, Bobby must tell them the truth and ask to be forgiven. After that was accomplished, Fergus promised his son, they would set about finding

Berry, and if she was being ill used they would try to get her back.

But meantime a new pony was needed, and was bought, and by now he was as loved and spoiled as Berry had been.

"And you made this long trip," I said, "just to see that Berry was in a good home?"

"Aye. And I'm convinced that she couldn't have a better one." Fergus set aside his long-empty tea mug and struggled up out of the soft, low chair. "And now I expect Dapples and I had better be on our way, or we won't be home by milking time."

I went on riding Berry long after I'd grown too tall to look right on her. There were other horses who demanded my time, too, more and more of them as Dad's training business expanded and as I grew into a full partnership with him.

But none of the others, even those that I owned, was ever mine in the way that Berry was. We spent hours together in her box or on the roads, or on summer-scented paths through the beech wood. We grew so attuned to one another that our very moods were shared. If she was feeling overfed and lazy, I found myself content to dawdle along. If I was grouchy or depressed, as I often was during my teen years,

Berry seemed to put herself out to cheer me. She would lip at my face, or at my toes if I was riding her, until she made me laugh, and then we settled in to enjoy our ride.

One day I was sitting in school, paying a reasonable amount of attention to the lesson, when suddenly a picture came into my head, and a great uneasiness. I saw Berry standing by a tree, the same tree she had tried to knock me off against. Her head was twisted at an odd angle, and she was in distress.

I jumped up, yelled something to the teacher about trouble at home, and ran.

When I reached the tree, there was Berry standing just as I'd seen her. She had apparently been rubbing her head against the tree to scratch an itch, and her halter had got caught over a bit of tough creeper vine that grew around the tree trunk. I released her, and felt her relief and gratitude flooding through me.

I'll confess something I've never told anyone before. Dad had wanted to breed Berry and raise a colt from her. He wanted to breed her to a little thoroughbred he knew, and try for a good polo pony prospect. I wouldn't let him.

I was afraid that I would share Berry's pain

at foaling time. I believe that I was even a little bit afraid that she might die in foaling, as her dam had done, and that if she did, something dreadful would happen to me, too.

Of course she did die eventually, in her sleep as Terrance had done, but not before she'd helped me raise my own three boys.

I wonder if Berry will be there to greet me on the other side, when I die?